MARCH OF THE HUNDRED BEASTS

Other books in the series:

DINOSAUR COVE

MARCH OF THE ARMOURED BEASTS

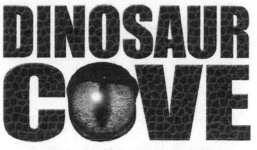

by
REX STONE

illustrated by
MIKE SPOOR

OXFORD
UNIVERSITY PRESS

With special thanks to Jane Clarke

To all my SCBWI friends

OXFORD
UNIVERSITY PRESS

Great Clarendon Street, Oxford OX2 6DP
Oxford University Press is a department of the University of Oxford.
It furthers the University's objective of excellence in research, scholarship,
and education by publishing worldwide in

Oxford   New York

Auckland   Cape Town   Dar es Salaam   Hong Kong   Karachi
Kuala Lumpur   Madrid   Melbourne   Mexico City   Nairobi
New Delhi   Shanghai   Taipei   Toronto

With offices in

Argentina   Austria   Brazil   Chile   Czech Republic   France   Greece
Guatemala   Hungary   Italy   Japan   Poland   Portugal   Singapore
South Korea   Switzerland   Thailand   Turkey   Ukraine   Vietnam

Oxford is a registered trade mark of Oxford University Press
in the UK and in certain other countries

© Working Partners Limited 2008
Illustrations © Mike Spoor 2008
Eye logo © Dominic Harman 2008

Series created by Working Partners Ltd

The moral rights of the author have been asserted

Database right Oxford University Press (maker)

First published 2008

British Library Cataloguing in Publication Data

Data available

ISBN: 978-0-19-272094-8

1 3 5 7 9 10 8 6 4 2

Printed in Great Britain by Cox and Wyman Ltd, Reading, Berkshire

FACT FILE

▷ JAMIE HAS JUST MOVED FROM THE CITY TO LIVE IN THE LIGHTHOUSE IN DINOSAUR COVE. JAMIE'S DAD IS OPENING A DINOSAUR MUSEUM ON THE BOTTOM FLOOR OF THE LIGHTHOUSE. WHEN JAMIE GOES HUNTING FOR FOSSILS HE MEETS A LOCAL BOY, TOM, AND THE TWO DISCOVER A WORLD WITH REAL LIVE DINOSAURS! TRACKING DINOSAURS IS EXCITING, BUT DANGER SURROUNDS THE BOYS AT EVERY TURN.

JAMIE

- **FULL NAME:** JAMIE MORGAN
- **AGE:** 8 YEARS
- **SIZE:** 1 JATOM*
- **TOP SPEED:** 10 KPH
- **LIKES:** FOSSIL HUNTING AND LEARNING ABOUT DINOSAURS
- **DISLIKES:** BEING STUCK INDOORS

Jamie's eye

Jamie's foot

Jamie's hand

*NOTE: A JATOM IS THE SIZE OF JAMIE OR TOM: 125 CM TALL AND 27 KG IN WEIGHT

TOM

- **FULL NAME:** THOMAS CLAY
- **AGE:** 8 YEARS
- **SIZE:** 1 JATOM*
- **TOP SPEED:** 10 KPH
- **LIKES:** TRACKING ANIMALS AND EXPLORING WILDLIFE
- **DISLIKES:** RAINY DAYS

Tom's eye   Tom's hand

WANNA

- **FULL NAME:** WANNANOSAURUS
- **AGE:** 65 – 80 MILLION YEARS**
- **SIZE:** LESS THAN A JATOM*
- **TOP SPEED:** 50 KPH, ESPECIALLY WHEN BEING CHASED BY A T-REX
- **LIKES:** STINKY GINGKO FRUIT AND BANGING HIS HEAD ON TREE TRUNKS
- **DISLIKES:** SCARY DINOSAURS

Wanna's head   Wanna's foot

*NOTE: A JATOM IS THE SIZE OF JAMIE OR TOM: 125 CM TALL AND 27 KG IN WEIGHT
**NOTE: SCIENTISTS CALL THIS PERIOD THE LATE CRETACEOUS

ANKYLOSAURUS

Ankylosaurus' eye

Ankylosaurus' spikes

Ankylosaurus' Tail

Ankylosaurus' foot

- **FULL NAME:** ANKYLOSAURUS
- **AGE:** 65 – 80 MILLION YEARS**
- **HEIGHT:** 2 JATOMS*
- **LENGTH:** 9 JATOMS*
- **WEIGHT:** 150 JATOMS*
- **LIKES:** GOBBLING GREENERY AND PRODUCING GAS
- **DISLIKES:** GETTING STUCK IN THE MUD

*NOTE: A JATOM IS THE SIZE OF JAMIE OR TOM: 125 CM TALL AND 27 KG IN WEIGHT
**NOTE: SCIENTISTS CALL THIS PERIOD THE LATE CRETACEOUS

DINOSAUR COVE

Village

Marina

SealighT Head

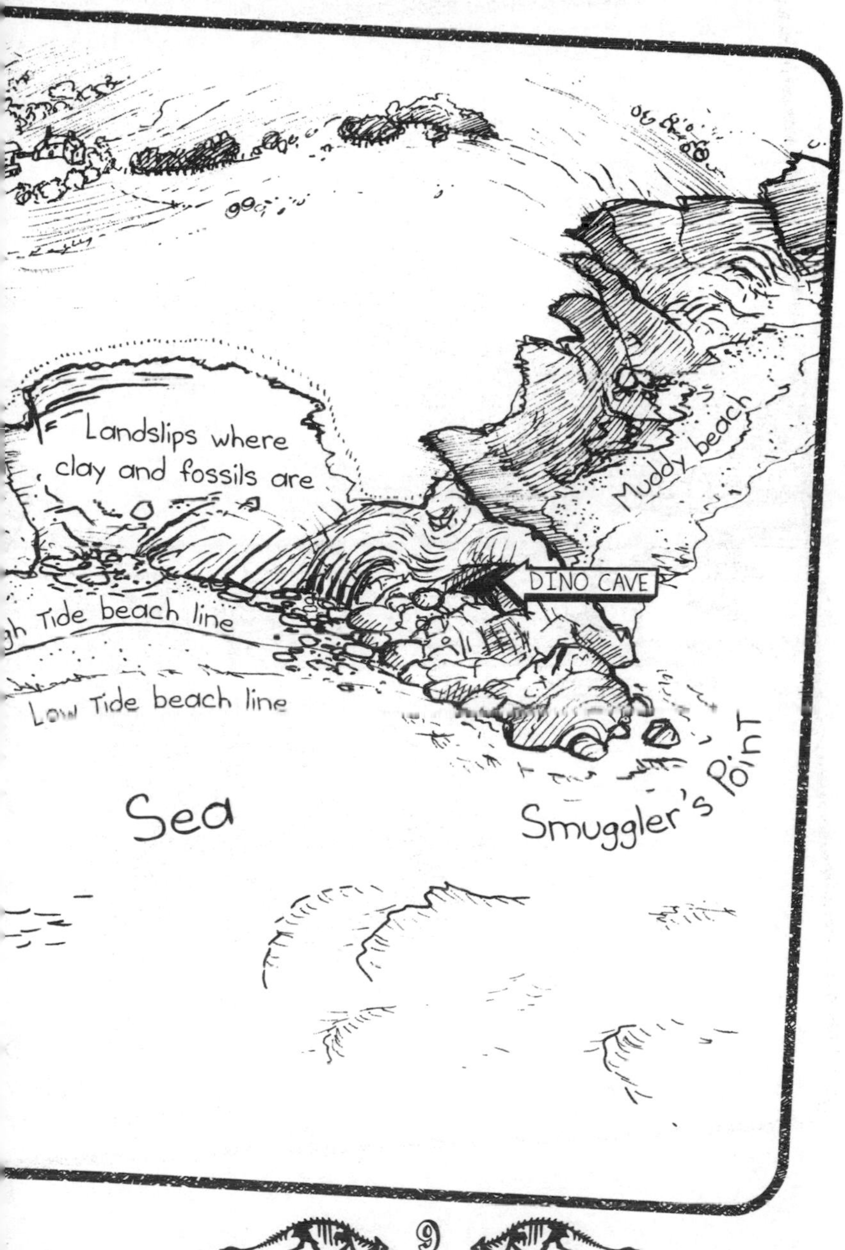

Landslips where clay and fossils are

High Tide beach line

Low Tide beach line

Sea

Muddy beach

DINO CAVE

Smuggler's Point

CHAPTER 1

Jamie picked out a small fossil from the heap of gooey mud that had slipped down onto Dinosaur Cove beach in the night. The stone looked like a stubby pencil with a sharp point. He wiped it on his jeans and handed it to his best friend Tom.

'That could be a dinosaur tooth,' Jamie's grandad said, putting down his fishing bucket and leaning in for a closer look.

'It's not a dinosaur tooth,' Tom replied. 'They don't look anything like this in real li—'

Jamie nudged Tom with his elbow. Grandad didn't know they'd discovered real live dinosaurs through a secret cave in Dinosaur Cove.

'Let's find out what it is.' Jamie rummaged inside his backpack. 'Compass . . . cheese and pickle sandwiches . . . Fossil Finder!' Jamie flipped open the lid of the hand-held computer and typed 'stubby pencil' in the search box. At once a picture of the fossil popped up.

'*BEL-EM-NITE*,' he read. '*THIS BULLET-SHAPED FOSSIL IS THE BODY OF A SEA CREATURE LIKE A SQUID.*' Jamie snapped the Fossil Finder shut and put it, and the belemnite, in his backpack.

'Fossil squid, eh?' Grandad chuckled. 'You can't eat those! I'm off to find some *fresh* fish.'

'And we should go find some fresh dinosaurs,' Tom whispered to Jamie as Grandad gathered up his fishing gear.

'Don't get stuck in the mud!' Grandad's eyes twinkled as he turned towards the sea. 'It'll swallow you up and spit out your bones, just like it did to the dinosaurs . . . '

The instant Grandad was out of hearing range, the boys yelled, 'Dino World here we come!'

They dashed towards the path that led from the beach up to the smugglers' cave where the hidden entrance to Dino World was. At the bottom of the path, Jamie spotted two large footprints in the sand.

Jamie skidded to a halt. 'Wait, Tom. Someone has been here!'

Tom bent down to examine the shoe imprints. 'They're fresh,' he said, 'and they're leading up our path!'

'Oh no,' Jamie groaned. 'What if someone's found the way through our cave into Dino World?'

'Then it wouldn't be our secret any more,' Tom said grimly. 'You know grown-ups. They'd sell tickets to visitors to make money out of it.'

Jamie frowned. 'Or they'd say it was dangerous and close

it up completely. We might never get to go back!'

Jamie and Tom examined the ground carefully and followed the footprints up the steep slope to the pile of boulders beneath their secret cave.

'Someone definitely came this way,' Jamie said.

'We've got to make sure the cave's safe.' He clambered up the boulders as fast as he could.

'What are you waiting for?' he called from the top. Tom was lingering over a footprint beneath the boulders. Jamie hopped impatiently from one foot to another as Tom scaled the boulders and hauled himself up next to Jamie.

'There's no need to panic.' Tom grinned and led the way into the cool cave. 'No one came in here. Those footprints went on past the boulders. Our cave is safe!'

'But what if they come back?' Jamie flicked on his torch and shone it into the corner of the cave. The light disappeared into the gap they'd discovered on their first visit.

'Stop worrying,' Tom told him. 'There's no way someone with feet that big could get through here.'

'You're right.' Jamie breathed a sigh of relief as he pushed his backpack through the tiny gap and crawled in after it, followed closely by Tom.

He flashed his torch over the floor of the secret chamber and picked out the fossilized footprints

of their dinosaur friend,
Wanna, which had led
them twice into Dino World.

'That foot wouldn't fit in these
tracks, either.' Jamie stepped into the first
of the small clover-shaped prints in the solid
rock. 'But they're exactly the right size for us!'

'Then let's track dinosaurs!' Tom declared.
'I'm right behind you.'

'One . . . two . . . three . . . ' Jamie's heart
beat faster as he counted each step. *What kind
of dinosaurs will we see today?* he wondered.

' . . . four . . . '

The cave wall in front of him looked like
solid rock, but as he put his foot forward a
crack of light appeared.

'FIVE!'

The crack of light widened and the ground
felt soft under Jamie's trainers as he stepped
from the dark cave into Dino World.

CHAPTER 2

Jamie stood blinking in the sunlight as the familiar smells of wet leaves and stinky gingko fruit filled his nose. A moment later, Tom was standing next to him on Gingko Hill.

'Wanna! Here, Wanna!' Jamie raised his voice above the buzzing insects and the calls of creatures in the steamy jungle.

'That's strange,' Tom said. 'He usually comes right away.'

'Maybe we could track him,' Jamie wondered aloud.

Jamie and Tom examined the ground outside the cave for traces of their faithful dinosaur friend and saw fresh footprints—just like the fossilized ones back in the cave—leading down the side of Gingko Hill.

'Wanna's gone south, down the hill,' Tom said, looking at his compass. 'We've never been that way before. Let's follow him!'

'Hang on a minute.' Jamie picked some smelly gingko fruit and put them in his backpack. 'For Wanna when we see him.'

Then the boys hurried down the hill.

'This is steep!' Jamie said as his legs picked up speed.

'Beat you to the bottom!' Tom yelled.

Jamie raced his friend down the hill, skidding and sliding, grabbing at trailing vines and low branches to keep from falling head over heels.

Jamie leaped down the last little way to land in the soft mud at the base of the hill.

Splat!

'I was first!' puffed Jamie as mud slopped over the top of his trainers.

'No, I was first!' gasped Tom.

A glob of mud plopped off his curly red hair and splattered onto his freckly nose.

They looked at each other and laughed.

'Shh!' said Tom. 'I can hear a squishing noise.'

Jamie listened for a moment and then whirled round as a wet, sandpapery tongue licked his cheek.

'Yuck!' he yelled.

'It's Wanna!' Tom cheered.

The little green and brown dinosaur wagged his tail, splattering mud all over them. Then he cocked his bony head to one side and looked hopefully at Jamie's backpack.

'Here you are, Wanna.' Jamie handed Wanna a stinky gingko fruit.

The little dinosaur grunked happily as he gobbled up the fruit, then he bounded up to Tom.

'Urgh, stinko breath! Aargh!' Tom landed on his back in the mud with Wanna on top of him, licking his face.

The mud squelched as Tom wrestled with Wanna. Jamie looked at the ground more closely. It was churned up and rutted as far as he could see.

'Stop mucking about!' he told Tom. 'We're standing in the middle of a dinosaur trackway.'

'What do you mean?' Tom asked, disentangling himself from Wanna.

'Look at all these footprints. A group of big, heavy dinosaurs have made this path.' Jamie pointed to a clear footprint at the edge of the track. He stepped on the mud next to it. The dinosaur footprint was over twice as long and much, much deeper than his. Jamie and Tom bent down and looked carefully at the print. There were four bumps for toes at the front.

'They're all heading that way.' Jamie pointed the way the toes were facing.

Tom wiped his muddy face with the sleeve of his T-shirt. 'Let's track them!'

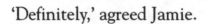

'Definitely,' agreed Jamie.

They trudged off along the muddy trackway with Wanna squishing along beside them. Suddenly, Wanna froze, his tail sticking out straight behind him.

The boys stopped and listened. For a moment there was silence, and then strange dinosaur calls began to boom down the trackway.

Aroop! Aroop! Aroooop!

'They sound like foghorns!' Jamie shuddered as the creepy calls echoed around them. Chills were running up and down his spine.

'Are we sure we want to catch up with those dinosaurs?' Tom asked nervously. 'What if they're meat eaters?'

'Good point.' Jamie wiped his muddy hands on his T-shirt, and took the Fossil Finder out of his backpack. He flipped it open and tapped in: DINOSAUR TRACKS, FOUR TOES.

'FOSSIL FOOTPRINTS ARE RARER THAN FOSSIL BONES,' he read. 'ROUNDED FOOTPRINTS WITH FOUR TOE MARKS AT THE FRONT WERE MADE BY HEAVY PLANT EATERS.'

Tom beamed. 'Dinosaurs here we come!'

CHAPTER 3

As Jamie, Tom, and Wanna followed the
trackway, the trees began to thin out and the
ground got wetter. Jamie's footsteps sank
deeper and deeper into the mud and a thin
fog drifted around them.

Even though they'd left the jungle behind,
the tracks stayed at the same width. 'These
dinosaurs are walking in a line,' Tom realized.

'Like elephants in those wildlife
documentaries.' Jamie said, as he leapt over a
giant purple and orange mushroom.

'How many are there?'
Tom asked.

'I can't tell,' Jamie said,
as his sodden jeans flapped
around his legs. 'They've
stomped all over each
other's tracks. Maybe a
T-Rex was chasing them?'

'I don't think so,' Tom
said. 'If they were running,
we'd see their toes digging
into the ground. They're
on a steady march.'

'Like an army!' Jamie
said, pausing beneath a
tree with moss dripping
from its twisted branches.
He peered through the
thickening mist. A fresh,
salty, tangy smell filled the

foggy air. Wanna took a
deep sniff and sneezed.

'This must be a marsh where
the river widens out and joins the ocean,'
Tom said.

Jamie narrowed his eyes. Strange
shapes were moving through the murk
like ghosts. Dinosaur calls echoed
across the marshland.

'Spooky!' Jamie shuddered.

'It's OK. They're plant eaters,
remember?' Tom squelched off into the mist,
followed by Wanna. Jamie watched as their

 31

footprints filled up with
bright green slime
the instant they'd made
them. He bent down and
looked more carefully at
the sludgy tracks. A series
of puddle footprints that

looked like smaller versions of the dinosaur
prints they were tracking branched off from
the path. He followed them as they zigzagged
through the marsh.

'Hey, Tom!' he called.

Tom didn't reply. Jamie peered through the
fog. He listened, but all he could hear were

33

the swarms of insects and the plopping and
gurgling of the marsh.

'Tom?' he yelled. 'Wanna?'

Jamie swallowed hard; he was all alone.

At last he heard a familiar noise.

Grunk, grunk!

'Wanna!' Jamie breathed a sigh of relief.

Wanna bounded out of the mist and licked
Jamie's cheek. Tom splashed after him.

'Wanna sniffed you out,' he explained. 'I
thought you were tracking the herd behind me.'

'I was following these baby tracks,' Jamie
said, pointing them out to Tom. 'It must have
wandered off on its own.'

'Babies should stay close to the adults for
protection.' Tom frowned. 'That baby could
be easy pickings for a predator. We should
help it get back to its herd!'

'In this fog?' Jamie asked. As he spoke, he
felt a breeze on his face and the fog tumbled

across the marsh, lifting a little. Wanna
snuffled happily around the slime pools
towards a plant with rubbery-looking leaves
and bright yellow flowers the size of dinner
plates.

'The bog doesn't worry Wanna,' Tom said.
'We'll be OK if we're careful.'

They watched as Wanna grabbed a flower
in his mouth, pulled it off and chewed it up.

Then he bounded back to the boys with his nose covered in yellow pollen.

'Tasty?' Jamie asked him.

Wanna wagged his tail.

'Perhaps those flowers tempted the baby away from the herd,' Tom said.

'Let's try and find him,' Jamie said and picked his way across the marsh following the baby footprints, trying to avoid the bright green sludge.

'It definitely came this way.' Tom pointed to a torn up patch of flowers.

As Jamie looked up, he tripped on a rock half-buried in the mud and staggered forwards, sinking up to his shins in a pool of green sludge.

'Urgh! This mud stinks of rotten eggs.' Jamie tried to step back onto the firmer ground, but his feet wouldn't move.

Bluurp!

The slime bubbled up to his knees.

'Uh oh,' Jamie said, struggling to move.
'I'm sinking into the bog!'

CHAPTER 4

Jamie tried again to pull his legs free from the bog, but it didn't help. Now, the mud was up to his thighs.

'Stop moving!' Tom yelled. 'You'll sink even quicker if you thrash around. You've got to lie down!'

Jamie looked down at the liquid mud swirling around his legs. 'You're joking.'

'You have to spread out your body weight,' Tom said urgently. 'It's the only way to get yourself out!'

Jamie took a deep breath and then threw himself flat in the revolting green goo. Slime oozed into his mouth, ears, and nose, but at least he stopped sinking. 'It's working!' he spluttered as he crawled out onto the firm ground by the marsh plant and stood dripping.

'This place is dangerous!' he told Tom. 'We should go back.'

'We can't go back, yet,' Tom said. 'Listen!'

Jamie scooped out the slime from his ears. Now he could hear a pitiful wailing echoing across the bog.

Aooo, aooo, aooo!

It was coming from behind a curtain of creepers that hung from the branches of a stunted tree. Jamie and Tom walked carefully towards the sound, jumping over the bright green patches of sinking slime. At the stunted tree, Wanna stopped to munch on another patch of yellow marsh plants.

The boys parted the creepers and saw a dinosaur the size of a small car up to its belly in the sludge. It was covered in thick bony plates from the tip of its beaky nose to the enormous club at the end of its tail. Two rows of spikes ran down its wide body and large horns stuck out from the back of its head. It looked at them mournfully and opened its mouth.

Aoo-ooo, it wailed, thrashing its club against the trunk of the tree. Splinters of rotten wood splattered into the marsh.

'What is it?' Tom asked.

Jamie was already tapping words '*BONY PLATES, SPIKED TAIL*' into the Fossil Finder.

'*AN-KY-LO-SAUR-US*,' he read. '*AN ARMOURED DINOSAUR AS STRONG AS A TANK. THIS SMALL-BRAINED DINOSAUR ATE TOUGH PLANTS AND PROBABLY PRODUCED GREAT QUANTITIES OF GASEOUS WASTE.*'

Jamie snapped the Fossil Finder shut and returned it to his backpack. He looked at the baby dinosaur.

'This anky is small-brained, all right. The more it thrashes its tail, the faster it sinks in the mud!'

'A bit like you, then!' Tom grinned.

Jamie threw a glob of mud at him.

Aooo-oooo! the baby wailed. Wanna started to grunk in sympathy. The anky thumped its tail against the stinky sludge.

'How are we going to get it out?' Jamie sighed.

'We'll have to calm it down first,' Tom said. 'But how do you calm down a dinosaur?'

Jamie looked at Wanna, whose nose was still plastered in pollen. 'Feed it!'

Jamie took a handful of gingko fruit out of his backpack and tossed them, one by one, towards the baby anky. Wanna rushed in and gobbled them up as fast as Jamie could throw them. Then he dashed back to Jamie and stood dribbling and wagging his tail.

'We'll have to try something you don't like!' Jamie rummaged in his backpack and unwrapped the cheese and pickle sandwiches Grandad had made for their lunch.

Wanna sneezed and backed off, shaking his head and making *gak-gak* noises.

44

Jamie threw a sandwich under the baby anky's beak. It stopped thrashing its tail and sniffed suspiciously at it. Then it started to squeal as if it was being poisoned and began thrashing its tail again.

'Ankys don't like your grandad's pickle, either!' Tom said. 'What else can we try?'

'The marsh plant!' Jamie turned back to the marsh plants and wrenched off three large yellow flower heads. 'One for you, Wanna!'

Wanna pounced on it in delight.

Jamie skimmed the other two across the marsh like a frisbee. The baby dinosaur's long tongue flickered out and pulled a yellow flower into its mouth.

As it chewed, the anky's tail stopped thrashing.

'It's working! Let's get some more flowers.' Jamie bent to pick some more.

'Wait!' Tom said. 'Listen.'

A deep, mournful bellowing was coming from the other side of the tree.

Aroo! Aroo! Aroooo!

Jamie and Tom whirled round.

An enormous beaky head loomed out of the mist. The baby began squeaking excitedly.

'That must be the baby's mother,' Tom said.

The huge ankylosaurus lumbered slowly towards them.

'Awesome!' Jamie gasped. 'She's as big as a tank. And look at the size of that club at the end of her tail!'

The mum anky stopped. She stared at Jamie, Tom, and Wanna. Then she began to beat her clubbed tail into the marsh, sending up plumes of muddy spray.

'Uh oh,' Jamie whispered. 'She doesn't like us.'

Aroooomph! she snorted.

Wanna tried to hide behind Jamie.

'She's going to charge us!' Tom yelled.

'Run!'

CHAPTER 5

The boys and Wanna darted behind the twisted tree trunk.

'What's happening?' Tom asked.

Jamie peered out.

'She's not charging! She must know she'll get stuck if she comes any closer.' He looked over to the baby anky. It had stopped squealing and thumping its tail.

Maybe there is still a chance to help it, Jamie thought.

Tom crept out from the cover of the tree.

'The poor thing's stopped thrashing,' he said. 'It's exhausted!'

'We can get close to it now,' Jamie said. 'Perhaps we can push it out.'

'It's worth a try,' Tom agreed. 'As long as the mum will let us.'

The boys picked their way round to the back of the baby.

'OK,' said Jamie. 'The ground's solid here.

Be careful not to step into the slime and watch out for that tail! One, two, three . . . heave!'

They pushed as hard as they could, but the baby dinosaur didn't budge.

Beneath the anky's armoured bottom, the swamp began to gloop and burble. There was a loud whooshing noise and the surface of the slime boiled.

Plop! *Plop! Plop!*

The bubbles burst, splattering their faces with gunge.

A hideous smell welled up around them. Jamie coughed and gagged. It was even worse than rotten eggs.

'What's that smell?' Tom gurgled. His face was dripping with green slime.

'Anky gas!' Jamie gagged. 'It farted!'

'I didn't know baby ankys had rocket boosters,' Tom gasped, fanning at the air.

'They'd be easier to get out of the bog if they did.' Jamie grimaced. 'One more try!'

The baby anky didn't move.

'It's like trying to push a truck,' Jamie groaned.

'That's what we need,' said Tom. 'A truck to pull it out of the swamp.'

'Or a tank . . . ' Jamie looked across at the mum ankylosaurus and thought hard. 'We might not have a truck or a tank,' he said, 'but we do have the next best thing.'

Tom grinned. 'You're right! Now all we need is some rope.'

The boys looked at each other.

'Creepers!' they yelled together, rushing back to the tree where Wanna was munching on marsh plants. He wagged his tail as they came up to him.

53

'No time to play,' Jamie told him. 'We're busy!'

Jamie and Tom heaved at the dangling creepers, but they didn't break off.

'It's good that they're strong,' Tom said. 'But we've got to get some down!'

'I'll climb up and cut some off.' Jamie shinned up a vine, straddled the branch and rummaged in his backpack, pulling out the fossil belemnite. 'I knew this would come in useful,' he muttered and used the fossil's sharp point to hack away at the vines.

As the creepers fell to the ground, Jamie swung back down to Tom.

Fisherman's knot

'We'll need to tie them together,' he told Tom. 'Do you know any good knots?'

Tom nodded. 'A fisherman's knot!' Tom showed Jamie how to do it.

Fig 1

Soon, they had three long lengths of vine. They twisted them together for strength, and made a big loop at each end.

Fig 2

'We'll need some treats,' Tom said. Wanna watched hopefully as the boys stuffed their pockets with the yellow marsh plant petals.

Fig 3

'Not for you,' Jamie told him. 'For the ankys.'

Fig 4

Wanna seemed a little disappointed.

'Now we've got to get these loops around the dinosaurs,' Jamie told Tom. The boys sloshed back to the baby anky and Tom dropped a flower for him to eat. Then Tom carefully threw his loop over the baby's head.

'That's the easy bit.' Jamie clutched the loop at the other end of the vines. 'Now for the mum . . . ' He pulled a handful of petals from his pocket and slowly approached her.

The mum anky fixed Jamie with her hooded eyes and lowered her head. Her tail beat the sludge, splattering him with stagnant water. Jamie threw a petal in front of her. She sniffed at it and ate it.

'So far, so good,' Jamie murmured. He crept closer and threw a whole handful of petals to the side. She twisted round to eat them.

'Watch out!' Tom yelled.
Jamie jumped out of the way as the club
on the end of the mum's tail whipped
past his head.

'Throw more flowers!' Tom called.
'Turn her right round.'

Jamie flung more petals on the marsh,
moving around to keep out of the way of the
clubbed tail. The mum anky turned and
began to graze. Jamie picked up the vine rope
and took hold of the loop.

He threw it, like a lasso, over her
shoulders, but it snagged on one of the horns.

'Missed!' Jamie muttered. The anky carried
on chewing peacefully on the petals.

58

'She hasn't noticed,'
Tom called.

'I'll unhook it and try again!'

Jamie crept towards her and took hold of the loop wedged behind her horn. He could feel the steam from her nostrils as he worked it free.

Suddenly the baby anky began to snort and wail.

Aroooph! The mum anky lifted her head, jerking Jamie off his feet. His wrist was caught in the vines!

Aroop, aroop, aroop!

The mum anky stumbled into the bog, with Jamie dangling from her neck. He struggled to get loose as her tail thrashed angrily, but he was stuck. Then the two front legs of the huge beast began to sink into the pool of sludge.

I'm doomed, Jamie thought. *Like Grandad said, the mud will swallow me up and spit out my bones!*

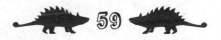

CHAPTER 6

Dangling just above the slime, Jamie realized that the safest place to be was on top of the dinosaur.

Pulling with all his might, he hauled himself up onto the back of the mum anky's neck. He untangled the loop from the horn, then quickly reached down over her head and slipped it around her neck.

Tom was gawping at him.

Jamie gave Tom the thumbs up sign and got unsteadily to his feet. His muddy trainers

got a grip on the anky's
rough plating and he turned
and ran along the anky's
thick neck and up over her
wide body between the two
rows of spikes. He sprang
off her back and landed
next to Tom.

'Awesome!' Tom
grinned. 'You just ran
over a dinosaur!'

'Better than a dinosaur running over me,'
Jamie said. 'Now all we've got to do is turn
her round again and get her to pull her baby
out. We'll need lots of petals for that!'

The boys gathered armfuls of the juiciest
looking marsh plants.

'Here, Anky!'
Jamie threw some
plants just out of reach
of the mum ankylosaurus.

The great beast lifted her
front legs out of the sludge,
moved slowly towards them and
began to chew.

'More!' Tom threw more petals in front
of her. As the mum strained towards them,
the length of vine attaching her to her baby
tightened.

'It's working!' Tom cheered as the mum
anky lurched forward onto dry land heaving
her baby out after her. The baby struggled to
its feet.

'Yes!' Jamie and Tom
leaped into the air to give
each other a high five as the
mum anky turned and touched
beaks with her baby.

'We'd better take off the vines,'
Jamie said.

'My turn!' Tom grinned. 'You keep them busy eating.'

Wanna bounded up, wagging his tail. He dropped a mouthful of petals at Jamie's feet.

'Thanks, Wanna, that's just what we need.' Jamie threw petals in front of the ankys' beaks. As they munched, Tom carefully unhitched the vines from their necks and slowly backed away.

The ankys stopped eating. They raised their heads together and made a soft high-pitched oooping noise.

'I think they're saying thank you!' Jamie said in amazement.

As Jamie, Tom, and Wanna watched, the mist thinned. The mum gently nudged her baby and they turned away from the boys. Ahead of them, a line of ankylosaurs was marching slowly onwards.

'It's the rest of their herd!' As Jamie spoke, the mum and baby lumbered over to the line calling *Aroop!*

The herd stopped and turned their heads. *Arooo! Aroo!* They lowed in reply as mum and baby caught up with them. The mum nudged her baby between the legs of the biggest ankylosaurus.

'That must be the dad,' Tom said.

The mum anky moved in behind him as the herd of armoured beasts continued its march.

Wanna grunked happily and turned back towards the trackway.

'Our first dino rescue,' Jamie said with satisfaction. 'But Wanna's right. It's time to go home.'

'You should see yourself!' Tom laughed as they trudged after Wanna. 'You're a sight!'

'Look who's talking!' Jamie grinned. Tom was covered from head to toe in stinky green marsh mud.

They trekked up Gingko Hill and stopped by Wanna's nest.

'We have to go back now, Wanna,' Jamie told him. He took the last of the gingko fruit out of his backpack.

Grunk grunk. Wanna wagged his tail and settled down happily to chew his treat.

'See you next time!'

Jamie stepped backwards through the dinosaur footprints, feeling the ground turn to stone under his feet. He was back in the cave, and a moment later Tom stood beside him.

Jamie shone his torch on Tom. The green slime that had covered him in Dino World had turned into a thick layer of dust.

He sniffed at the dust on his own T-shirt.

'Yuck!' he sneezed. 'It still stinks of marsh and anky gas. We'd better get it off before anyone notices.'

They squeezed back through the gap and scrambled down the boulders towards the beach. The tide was out. In the distance, Grandad waved and began to pick up his fishing gear. Jamie waved back.

'Beat you into the sea!' he challenged Tom.

The boys raced across the beach, threw themselves into the sea, and came up spluttering.

'I was first,' laughed Jamie.

'No, I was first,' grinned Tom.

They splashed water all over each other until they were sure they'd washed off every trace of ankylosaurus.

'Ahoy there, me hearties,' Grandad greeted them as they emerged dripping from the sea. 'It looks as if you've had fun today!'

'Great fun!' Tom said. 'But I'd better be getting home now. See you tomorrow, Jamie?'

'You bet!' Jamie waved as Tom set off for the village.

'What have you boys been up to?' Grandad asked Jamie as they walked up towards the lighthouse.

'We've been tracking dinosaurs!' Jamie told him. 'But don't worry, Grandad— we were careful. We didn't get stuck in the mud.'

Far Away Mountains

Crashing
Rock
Falls

Great Plains

Fang
Rock

Gingko
Hill

GLOSSARY

Ankylosaurus (an-ki-low-sor-us) – a vegetarian dinosaur known for its armoured coat and clubbed tail (see below). Its armour consisted of large bony bumps similar to the covering of modern-day crocodiles and lizards.

Belemnite (bell-em-nite) – an extinct squid-like sea creature. Belemnite had ten arms of similar length with small hooks and beak-like mouths. Its fossils usually only preserve the creature's bullet-shaped body.

Bog – wetlands with soggy, spongy ground that are often too soft to walk across.

Clubbed tail – the tail of an ankylosaurus which resembled a huge, armoured golf club. The ankylosaurus used its tail as a weapon and could break bones of its enemies with a swift swing.

Fisherman's knot – named for its usefulness to fishermen. Two knots are tied in two ropes lying side by side. Tie a knot in one rope and slip the other rope through the hole; then tighten. Do the same to the other rope.

Fossil Finder – hand-held computer filled with dinosaur facts.

Gingko (gink-oh) – a tree native to China called a 'living fossil' because fossils of it have been found dating back millions of years, yet they are still around today. Also known as the stink bomb tree because of its smelly apricot-like fruit.

Marsh – shallow wetlands that are almost continuously flooded by a variety of sources, including rain, streams, and the sea.

Predator – an animal that hunts and eats other animals.

Wannanosaurus (wah-nan-oh-sor-us) – a dinosaur that only ate plants and used its hard, flat skull to defend itself. Named after the place it was discovered: Wannano in China.

Look up!
I'll be flying
in soon ...